S0-FLO-149

Max Plants a Seed

A Book about the Life Cycle of a Sunflower

BY KERRY DINMONT

The Child's World®
childsworld.com

Published by The Child's World®
1980 Lookout Drive • Mankato, MN 56003-1705
800-599-READ • www.childsworld.com

Photographs ©: Shutterstock Images, cover, 1 (bottom), 1 (top), 16; iStockphoto, 3, 5, 13, 14; Ruta Saulyte-Laurinaviciene/Shutterstock Images, 6, 20; Bogdan Wankowicz/Shutterstock Images, 9, 10; ClarkandCompany/iStockphoto, 19

Design Elements: Shutterstock Images

Copyright © 2018 by The Child's World®
All rights reserved. No part of this book may be reproduced or utilized in any form or by any means without written permission from the publisher.

ISBN 9781503820340
LCCN 2016960938

Printed in the United States of America
PA02339

Today, Max plants a sunflower **seed**.

How will it grow?

5

6

Max plants the seed where it will get a lot of sunlight. He waters it.

The seed soaks up water. **Roots** start to grow out of the seed.

9

10

Then a **stem** grows out of the seed. This all happens under the soil.

The stem comes out of the soil 11 days after Max plants it. The stem is tiny.

13

14

The stem grows taller.

It starts to grow leaves.

16

A flower grows on the top. The flower makes hundreds of seeds!

Max collects the seeds.

He will plant seeds again next year.

19

20

What seeds would you like to plant?

Words to Know

roots (ROOTS) Root are the parts of a plant that grow into the soil. Roots soak up water and feed the plant.

seed (SEED) A seed is something made by a plant. A seed can grow into a new plant.

stem (STEM) A stem is the main part of a plant. Leaves grow on a stem.

Extended Learning Activities

⭐ 1 Can you think of other plants that make seeds? Do all seeds look alike?

⭐ 2 Have you ever planted a flower? What kind was it? How big did it grow?

⭐ 3 Why do you think seeds need water and sunlight to grow?

To Learn More

Books

Markovics, Joyce L. *Sunflower*. New York, NY: Bearport Publishing, 2016.

Rattini, Kristin Baird. *Seed to Plant*. Washington, DC: National Geographic, 2014.

Web Sites

Visit our Web site for links about sunflowers: childsworld.com/links

Note to Parents, Teachers, and Librarians: We routinely verify our Web links to make sure they are safe and active sites. So encourage your readers to check them out!

About the Author

Kerry Dinmont is a children's book author who enjoys art and nature. She lives in Montana with her two Norwegian elkhounds.

Children's 583.983 DIN
Dinmont, Kerry, 1982-
Max plants a seed : a
book about the life

02/13/18